E
ELL

5542

DATE DUE

JAN 2 5 1995		
OCT 21		
OCT 14		

Elliott, David

Dragon Tangle

DEMCO

Dragon Tangle

David Elliot

Ashton Scholastic

Auckland Sydney New York Toronto London

The author and the publisher wish
to thank the Literature Programme
of the QEII Arts Council for its
assistance in creating this book.

First published 1994

Ashton Scholastic Ltd
Private Bag 92801, Auckland 5, New Zealand.

Ashton Scholastic Pty Ltd
PO Box 579, Gosford, NSW 2250, Australia.

Scholastic Inc.
555 Broadway, New York, NY 10012, USA.

Scholastic Canada Ltd
123 Newkirk Road, Richmond Hill, Ontario L4C 3G5, Canada.

Scholastic Publications Ltd
7-9 Pratt Street, London NW1 0AE, England.

National Library of New Zealand
Cataloguing-in-Publication data

Elliot, David, 1952-.
    Dragon tangle / by David Elliot, Auckland, N.Z. : Ashton Scholastic, 1994.
    1 v.
    Children's picture story book told in rhyme.
    ISBN 1-86943-131-6
    I. Title.
        NZ823.2   zbn94-12206

9 8 7 6 5 4 3 2 1   4 5 6 7 8 9/9

Edited by Penny Scown
Printed in Hong Kong

For Mhairi

With thanks to Tania Atkinson
who started these dragons on this adventure

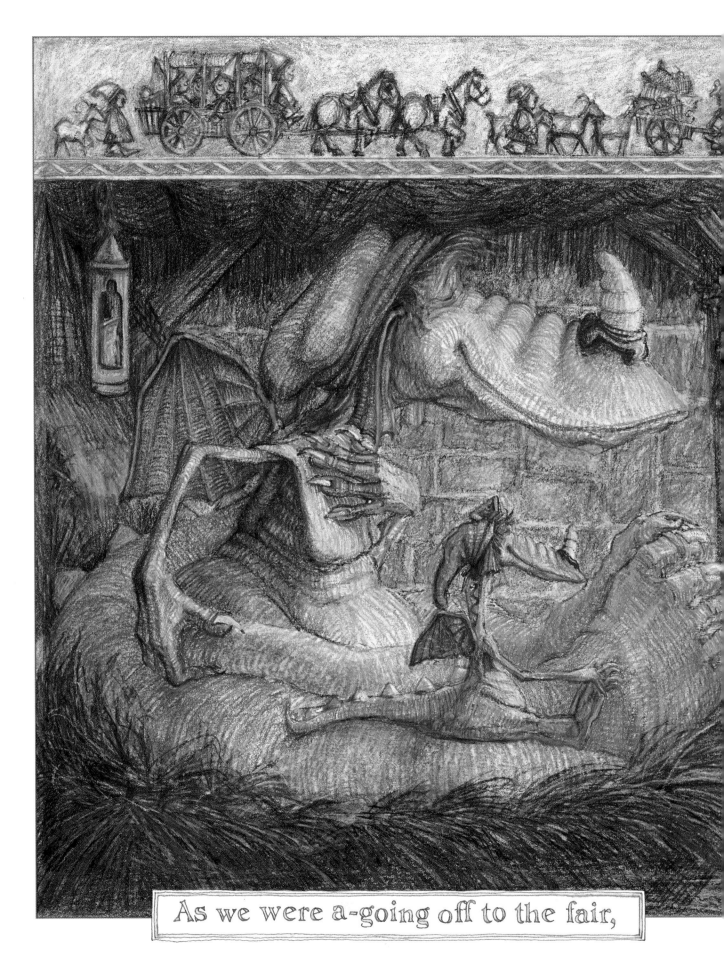

As we were a-going off to the fair,

who should jump up and follow us there?

Who squeezed themselves into Molly the Hatter's

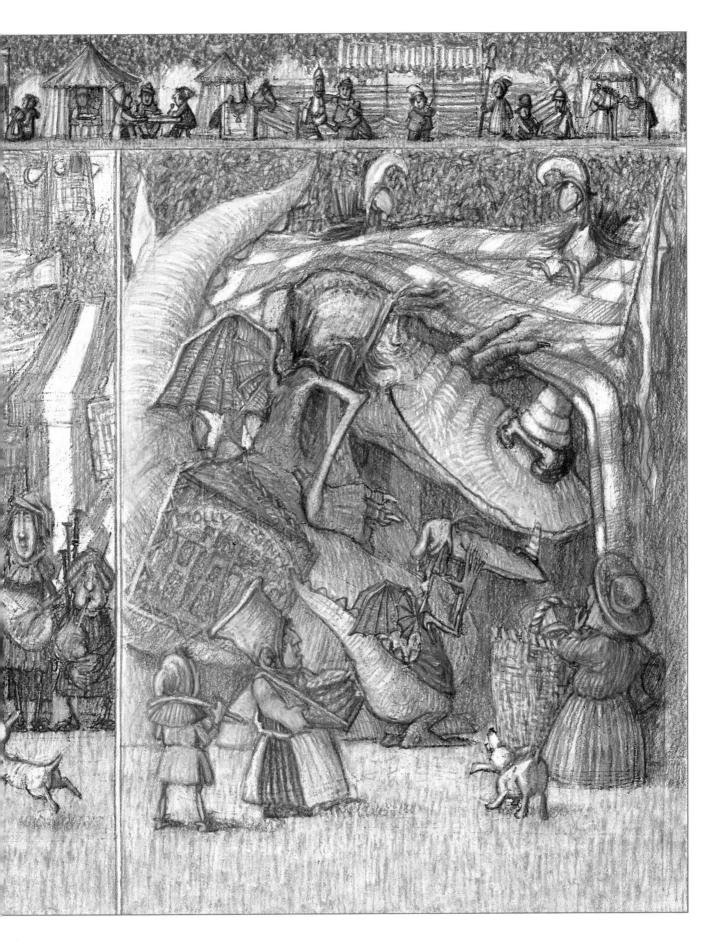

then stomped out leaving her tent in tatters?

Who bashed and bellowed behind Bob's band?

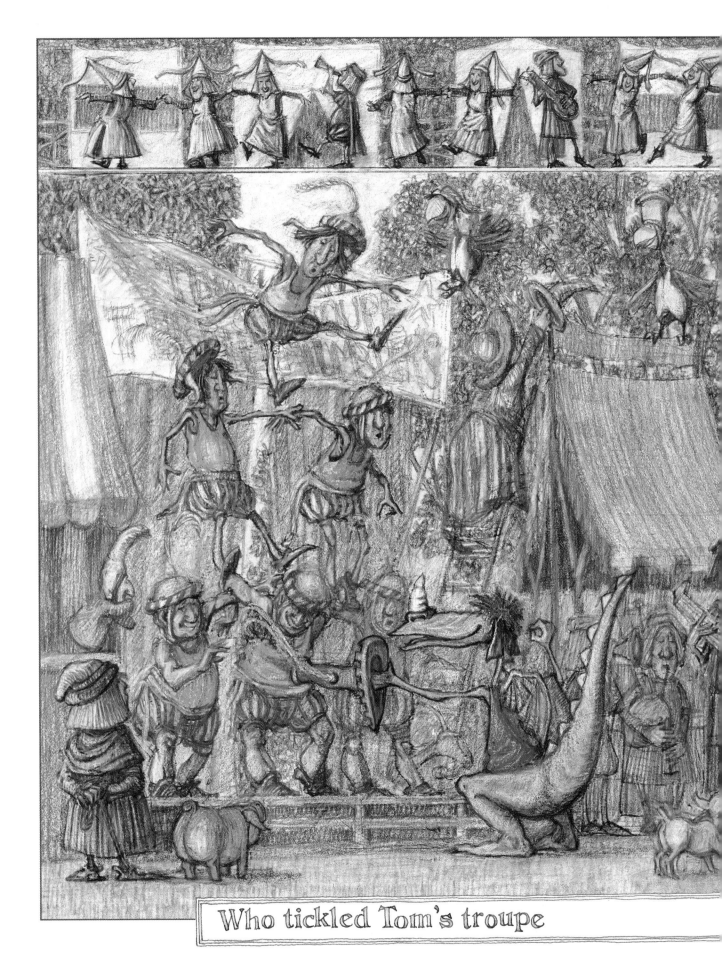

Who tickled Tom's troupe

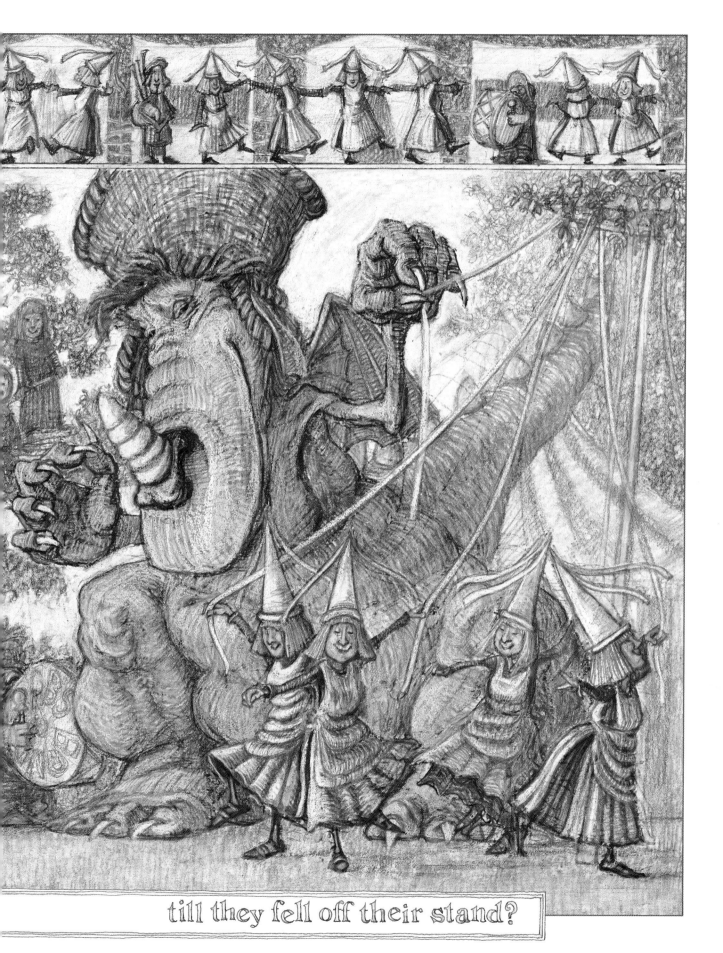

till they fell off their stand?

Who twirled the May girls into the skies?

Who squashed the pieman's puddings and pies?

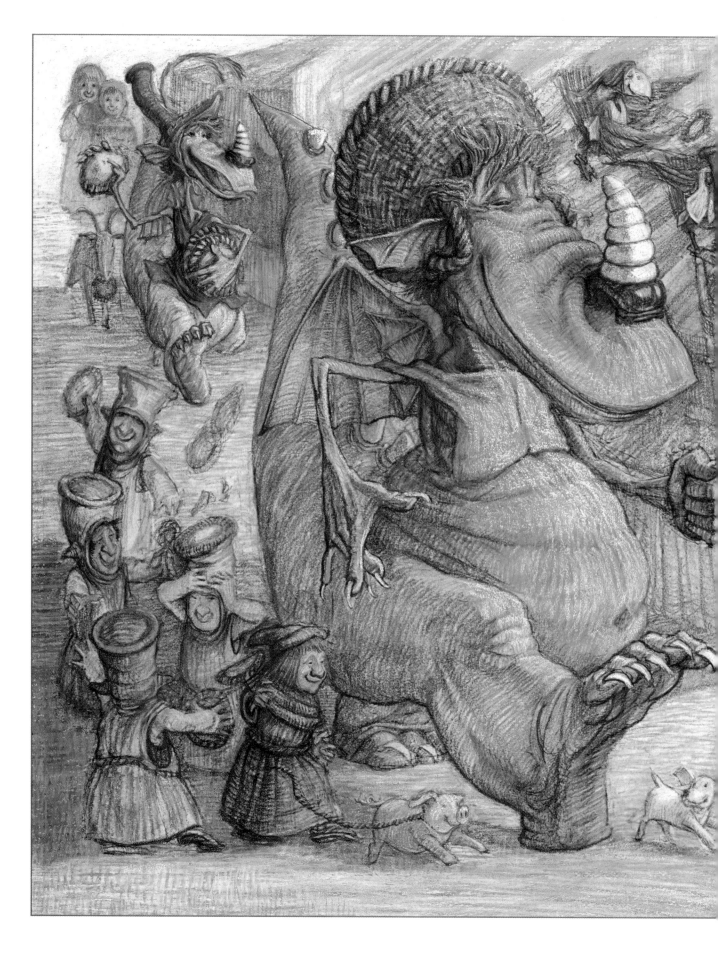

Who snaffled Sir Jasper and Sir John ...

from their horses and jousted on

most recklessly before the king?

Who tripped and got tangled in everything?

When the queen shouted stop, who wouldn't obey

Who didn't see poor Billy's cart ...

in the way?

And after all of the lolloping chasing-abouts,

and all of the bellows, the tangles, the shouts ...

Who were still friends? Who had not a care?

As we were a-going home from the fair?

Dragons!

So next time you're going off to the fair,
do watch out for dragons there!